MY BEST FRIEND

Pat Hutchins

MY BEST FRIEND

Greenwillow Books, New York

Gouache paints were used for the full-color art.
The text type is Mixage Medium.

Printed in Hong Kong by South China Printing Company (1988) Ltd.
First Edition   10 9

Library of Congress Cataloging-in-Publication Data
Hutchins, Pat (date)
My best friend / by Pat Hutchins.
p.   cm.
Summary: Despite differences in abilities, two little
girls appreciate each other and are ''best friends.''
ISBN 0-688-11485-7 (trade)   ISBN 0-688-11486-5 (lib.)
[1. Friendship—Fiction.]   I. Title.
PZ7.H96165My   1993
[E]—dc20   91-48354   CIP   AC

FOR

HARRY
POLLY
BEVERLEY
JULIE
JANIS
DAVID
EILEEN
SUE
HELEN
KAREN
CAROL
JUDITH
JENNY
ELLEN
ANDREW

AND ESPECIALLY
CLARA JANE OF LUMB BANK

My best friend is coming
to spend the night.
I'm glad she's my best friend.

My best friend knows how to run faster

and climb higher

and jump farther than anyone.

I'm glad she's my best friend.

My best friend can eat spaghetti with a fork
and doesn't drop any on the table.

My best friend knows how to paint good pictures and doesn't get fingermarks on the paper.

My best friend knows
how to untie her shoelaces

and how to do up the buttons on her pajamas.

My best friend knows how to read.

I'm glad she's my best friend.

My best friend thinks
there's a monster in the room.

But I know there isn't.

I know it's only the wind blowing the curtains.

And I know if I close the window,
the curtains won't blow.

"I'm glad you're my best friend,"
said my best friend.

Since the publication of *Rosie's Walk* in 1968, reviewers on both sides of the Atlantic have been loud in their praise of Pat Hutchins's work. Among her popular picture books are *Tidy Titch; What Game Shall We Play?; Where's the Baby?* (an *SLJ* Best Book of the Year); *The Doorbell Rang* (an ALA Notable Book); and *The Wind Blew* (winner of the 1974 Kate Greenaway Medal). For older readers she has written several novels, including *The House That Sailed Away, The Curse of the Egyptian Mummy,* and *Rats!* Pat Hutchins, her husband, Laurence, and their sons, Morgan and Sam, live in London, England.